SURVIVIN
PHILLY

NATE (NTG) JONES

authorHOUSE®

AuthorHouse™
1663 Liberty Drive
Bloomington, IN 47403
www.authorhouse.com
Phone: 1 (800) 839-8640

Published by AuthorHouse 11/30/2018

ISBN: 978-1-5462-7049-2 (sc)
ISBN: 978-1-5462-7048-5 (e)

Library of Congress Control Number: 2018914103

Print information available on the last page.

Any people depicted in stock imagery provided by Getty Images are models, and such images are being used for illustrative purposes only. Certain stock imagery © Getty Images.

This book is printed on acid-free paper.

DEDACATED IN LOVING MEMORY OF

MY MOTHER "NORREEN L JONES"
MY BROTHER "CLIFFORD W JONES"
AND MY BROTHER "ZOLLIE M JONES"
PEACE UNTIL WE MEET AGAIN

INTERLUDE

Yeah, I know you'll probably wonder why I'm headed this way on I-95. Well let's just say when you've been through what I've been through and you make it out you survive!!! Only advice I can give you is to keep it moving; just keep it moving'.

CHAPTER 1

It all started (June) summer of 05. It was a basic day, motherfucker trying to get at a dollar. Everything from loud, hard, pills, juice, you name it, you could get it.

Me and my young ins up top holding' it down, before you know it here comes TY. See, TY was this OG from back Summerville that ain't give a fuck. This motherfucker shot his Mom and her boyfriend because they didn't save him any food.

He did 10 years. When he comes on the block I know to expect some bullshit. Even though this nigga was crazy, he knew what it was with my team, but the rest of them better get low.

Ray: Red, I ain't with dis shit today real talk.
Red: Yo youngin' chill he ain't fucking with us, fuck him.
Ray: Yo, if he come over here...
Red: Chill.
TY: Who got weed?
(He repeats)
TY: Who got some tree?

The young bull Pete had to be the one to say something.

Pete: I do. What you want OG?

TY: Let me get a dime of that Kush.

Soon as Pete went to the stash TY followed him and rushed him and took all his shit, went in his mouth, and in his pockets.

Now the young bull Pete ain't no bitch, he will pop that thing, and I knew shit was about to get crazy.

Ring, Ring (phone rings)
Red: Who dis?
Show: Nigga, its show.

Now Showboat was strictly about that Mugga. Don't get me wrong, he rock out if need be, but he mostly be chasing' that money. So I knew what this call was about.

Red: Yo Showboat. What it do big-time? Tell me something good!
Show: Everything good. I got them things. For ten flat! Only for you! Anybody else I need 13-5, you dig?
Red: Dam baby, that's love! Look, let me do my two step and I'm right at you.
Show: Say no more.

Now what I needed to do was make a few calls, touch a few people, so you know I called Dame. Dame was that dude in South Philly. He had shit pippin'. If it was going down he had his hand in it! And I called Stacy. Stacy was this bad ass stripper jawn from uptown and trust me, this bitch get at a dollar and will pull that heat. I told them both I got em for 12-5; get my break down, plus. I'm Coppin' one for myself as well.

(Later that day)

Ring, Ring (Phone rings)

Red: Yo Cuz?

Dame: Yo Red, ima need two of them things ASAP.

Red: ok got you, that's 25K.

Dame: Bet, Tell me when and where.

Soon as I hang up the phone with Dame, Stacy called me she and her squad wanted three pies at 37.5.

Now let's do the math. So that's 50 stacks for Showboat and 12.5 that I come up on! Now I can cop myself one pie and still have $2500 cash and I never have to come out of my pocket.

Its Tuesday, 8:45am quiet on the block, only a few heads up this early! Half of them never went in the house the night before. Yo! Motherfuckers will stay out for three, four days for that money! Shit was pippin'! Me, Ray, Pete, and Lil' Key was sitting at the crib on C- Block. I'm eating turkey bacon, egg and cheese drinking that good OJ. These niggas drinking 800 and smoking tree, SMFH, but that's what they do. Pete been up for two days chasing' these crack heads! He had to pay his lawyer trying' to beat this nut ass case he caught running up in niggas cribs, cars, and stores on some major BNE bullshit second case in one year. Some people got to learn the hard way. He was still hot over that five bomb bitch ass TY got him for two hundred in cash like three in that good Kush "he swollen" out of nowhere Ray hollered "I'm hungry as shit(crushing his beer can) walk me to the poppy store so I can get one of them fucking egg sandwiches."

Pete: Yeah, I can use one of them myself.

Red: Fuck it! I'll walk with you'll! Niggas strapped up, we out the door. We left Lil KEY at the spot to hold it down. Soon as we stopped on the porch who the first motherfucker you think I see? Yeah, TY! I'm hoping Pete don't see him cause I know how he ride. He got this big ass dumb looking 9mm on his waist, drunk off 800, ain't slept in days, stressing' over money this nigga took, and he's standing on the corner. It's too early for this shit! Now I'm trying to get them to walk the other way so he don't see him, but before I could say a word this nigga was on his way down the street with that look on his face. He grabbed his burner as he walked up on him.

Pete: TY!

(TY turned around.)

TY: Why the fuck is you calling my name like you fucking own me pussy? What the fuck do you want?

Pete: I want my fucking money!

TY: (Laughing) Bitch nigga you think I took that shit to give it back? You better get your bitch ass on before I trash you!

Before he could finish his last word Pete pulled and slapped the bullshit out of him with the burner, (opened him up to the white meat). TY fell to the ground but was still talking shit... Dig this, TY, he's like 6'5 250 lbs., while Pete is like 5'7 175lbs wet, but he got the heart of a bear, so to me it looked even!

Pete: Nigga where my money?

TY: Pussy, fuck you! Shoot me!

Why he say that? Pete shot him in the leg and asked him again. "Where's my fucking money?" Now TY, big ass bitchin' and screaming' like a fucking girl as Pete put the barrel to his head.

TY: Alright, I got you, I got you! Hold up!

Pete stepped back and let TY go in his pockets, he handed him like $160.

Pete took it, shot him in the other leg, and took off up the block. I sat there and watched as TY laid in street bleeding and cussing', talking all crazy and reckless bout what he going to do. (Fuck outta here). If he smart he will let that be a lesson and fall back, but I know it's not that simple. Now Pete knew he fucked up. See if you going to rock out on a nigga like TY, you better go all in cause he ain't letting' shit ride! He live for this type shit, and damn near died for it!!

It's only like 9:30 - 10:00 we got police everywhere, ambulance, fire trucks and every fucking neighbor out on the block. Shit, we ain't going to see no money today, so we shut down shop until it cooled off. I'm sitting' in the cut waiting for these nut ass cops to slide. They out there asking questions but ain't nobody telling them shit! FOH.

I hear somebody calling my name...

Ray: Red, Yo Red!
Red: Yo Ray.

He was sitting in the truck waving me on. (Ok we out) Ray was what we called a pretty boy. He was into money and hoes... (In that order) He could fight but he didn't have to. He would pay somebody to fuck you up or out you. He'd rather waste money on bitches than be beefing with a nigga! That's why I kept him around because he kept the hoes.

I jumped in the Tahoe. He was listening to "Official Swag" from the bull Twev. REDRUM RECORDS. We rocked out for a minute until my phone rung..."ring" I turned the radio down; it was Show on the other end.

Red: Yo Show I was just about to hit your jack got distracted by some dumb shit, but we good.

Show: So what them numbers looking' like?

Red: Six, so far!

Show: Say, word! When and where?

Red: Word! On my way to you know. You at the spot, or at the SPOT

Show: The spot, call when you get outside.

Red: Copy!

I look at Ray.

Red: I need you to take this run with me.

Ray: A run? What kind of run and what I get out this shit?

Red: I got to pick them things up! I got you. Ima take care of you.

Ray: Yeah! Motherfucker, take care of your boy... Where we going?

Red: Just keep straight I'll tell you where.

Showboat lived out in the Northeast, in the back of nowhere; I had to make Ray Park the car like four blocks away and wait while I walked just so this nigga Show wouldn't be bitchin. (Scary ass dude)

This nigga Showboat has been getting money for years. His family been getting money and put him in the game early. I grew up with them, so I guess he trusted me. I don't give a fuck, I don't trust anybody. The way it was out her anybody could get it.

I called his phone when I got a block away. He sent somebody out to meet me. When I got to the door I smelt the scent of incense and cigar smoke. All in all, it didn't smell bad, but when I stepped inside all I smelt was money.

Here this nigga go sitting at the table wearing' Gucci house shoes, a Gucci smoking jacket, smoking what smelt like a Cuban cigar. (Young Boss) He living' that life for real and I was all the way in!

CHAPTER 2

OPERATION FLOOD THE BLOCK

I sat and busted it up with SHOW for like a half hour (talking shit) I forgot I had RAY waiting in the car, but when I'm sitting around money I always seem to get comfortable, like that's where I belong! But I can't sit around smoking Cuban cigars, drinking Rosa' I had to get back to the streets so I can eat... So I'm like SHOW ima holla, wish I could stay longer and kick it but I got people waiting'. This motherfucka whistled, waved his hand and ol' boy came out the back with a black sack. He sat it on the table in front of SHOW and he opened it, showed me the six pies zipped the sack slide it across the table to me. I picked it up told him I'd holler later after I make my moves and I was out the door six bricks in a sack. I called RAY told him to meet me at the gas station at the corner of the block and we were out!!!

Now we need to ride from the northeast to South Philly so I can take the bul DAME his shit. First I needed to slide past my spot so I could put my pie on chill until I get back, no need to take it with me them South Philly dudes "grimiest"

So after dropping' my shit off we headed to SP, I called DAME he wants me to meet him at this fucking park at 23rd and REED shit don't seem rite but fuck it I guess we'll find out when we get there..

As we pulled up I could see DAME standing' outside talking with three dudes, from where I sit I don't think I know any of them, when DAME saw us he had this strange look on his face yet he still hollered out "RED" as if he was glad to see me.

I told RAY to stay in the truck, keep the engine running burner on lap. I got out but I left the black sack on the floor in the back… As I walked up I'm like wait two of these dudes look real familiar.

DAME: RED this is my West Philly squad, soon as he said that I remembered where I knew these dickheads from! These those fucking stick up boys!

DAME: This LIL, DIRT and LID it's one more name TOMMY but he wasn't with them at that time.

See the West Philly stick up boys are these Five-Six little young bulls that ride around the city robbing' everything moving', they got a black van with black limo tint, and they got a white van with black limo tint you never know where you might see them or how many of them might jump out on you. They hit a couple banks but for the most part their known for running' down on big time dope boys (These little niggas getting at that money) Crazy part is when I walked up they were talking' about the bul DIRT uncle TY said he got shot uptown back Summerville, talking' about some dude name PETE and what they gone do when they run into him.

I played my part like I ain't know who or what they're talking about, the young bul LID looked at me and said damn old head I know you from somewhere, I never said a word just raised my eye brows as to say OH YEAH??

They finished talking' to DAME then they got into a blue magnum wagon, in my mind I'm thinking' ok now I know what they drive on a normal (MENTAL NOTE TO SELF) Once they pulled off me and Dame conducted our business.

I had to run into the corner store to get a bag. The bitch behind the counter wants to charge me 25 cents for a regular black plastic bag that they gave away when you buy something. I'm like ok fuck it, take this quarter and give me a big bag.

I went back to the truck to separate Dame's two pies from Stacy's I walked back to the park and Dame reached for the bag. I pulled away. I'm like where the money cuz? He looked around then he pointed to the trash can. I guess Dame wasn't taking' no chances with stick up boys either. I went to the trash can looked in the bag and saw the cash and picked it up. I walked back to Dame and handed him the bag from the corner store with the two pies in it, then turned and walked straight back to the car. (Trust no one.)

RAY: Red, we good?
RED: Yes sir, we out.

He drove off. I started counting the money in the bag that I got from Dame, it was all there. I separated my money from the money I had to give to Showboat. I saw Ray watching' me as I was counting'.

RAY: Damn, O.G. its going' down

RED: Yea, if shit goes like I plan we're about to be on top!!

On the other side of town I had Stacy waiting' on me to drop off her work. She wanted me to meet her at 5th and Wyoming at the strip bar "Bottom's Up" when we arrived she was still working' so we sat and watched the show. Stacy was about 5'4, long black hair; pretty face… reminded me of a young ghetto Gabby Union. Her body was a 10, talking' bout nice, round full titties, thick hips and thighs, and an ass so fat it didn't even look real but trust me, it was. She was on stage dancing' to that new NTG shit "When She Do Dat" she had every man in the building hypnotized throwing' dollars and hollering' all types of crazy shit, but she was strictly about her money (no rap for nobody) she finished her set, picked her money up and went off the stage and made her way to the back. She looked back at me and gave me the nod to say come to the back. When I got up, every man in the building looked at me with envy.

I swaged to the back room full of half-naked bad ass bitches; most of them worked for or got their start from Stacy. Stacy stripped down naked right in front of me like it was nothing we talked while she got dressed. She turned around and I couldn't help but to slap that ass. She looked at me and said…

STACY: Ain't no free feels, next time Ima charge your ass.

RED: Yeah whatever (laughing).

Once she was dressed we went into a smaller room alone so we could get down to the business at hand. She went in her Coach bag and pulled out a fucking wad of money. Stacy handed me thirty stacks. She said wait as she went into her LV gym bag and counted out another six hundred. I tucked it then went into the black sack I carried like a book bag and gave her one brick at a time. She put them in the gym bag and did a little dance, kissed me on the cheek, and walked out!

When we returned to the front room RAY was in the corner getting a lap dance from this bad ass Rican jawn. When he noticed me looking at him he just smiled. I gave him the head nod to say we out he finished up and walked over to me.

RAY: We good.
RED: Yea, let's get the fuck out of here.

On our way back uptown me and Ray drove through Hunting Park to holla at my little cousin Gee. I and Gee used to get money up in HP before. I moved and I put him on. I left him the block so I always popped up to make sure he was good and showed my face.

When we pulled up on 8th street I saw Gee sitting' on the hood of his car talking' to the young ins my man Pete was also out there doing' his thing. This is the time I saw him since he shot the bul TY. We parked, got up and walked to where they were. I shook everybody's hand and gave love to my Lil' cousin then pulled Pete to the side.

PETE: What's the word up top? I heard that bitch ass TY supposed to be looking' for me.
RED: Yeah, he not going to let that ride, and you know this! You should have downed his ass, did us all a favor.
PETE: I know I fucked up, but fuck him, it is what it is! I'm like, Oh yeah, I was out South Philly earlier hollering'

at Dame. You know them stick up boys that b coming' through plotting on shit.

PETE: Yeah, I know them motherfuckers, what about them?

Dirt is the bull TY's nephew. He knows who I am. He was out South Philly talking' about some bull named Pete from Upt shot and robbed his uncle and he not gone rest until he get him.

PETE: Word?? Well them pussy's better come correct matter of fact I'm looking' for his ass now it's whatever (cocking his gun).

I talked to my cousin for a few and then we rolled out. Pete jumped in the car with me and Ray, but I need to drop them off somewhere so I can get this 60,000 to Showboat.

Riding' around with seventy thousand dollars cash and these crazy dudes; we all strapped and high, don't seem like a good idea. I hit Showboat and told him I'll be at you in an hour or so, all is good! He was like...

SHOW: You the fucking man, I got something for you my dude!

RED: Say no more.

Ray lived on Haines street (Uptown) with his BM; we went past there so he could handle some personal business. I told them to let Pete lay low and I needed to borrow the Tahoe for a couple hours.

RAY: No problem just put some gas in the tank.

RED: Done

Now that I am back on the truck alone I turned on the radio back on and zoned out to "BOSS" from NTG "Redrum Records".

I made it too Broad and Erie, when out of the corner of my eye I see that black van tinted out headed the opposite direction towards Somerville. I'm wondering who they going to fuck with tonight, hopefully Pete ass will listen to me and lay low at Ray house. It's like 11:40 pm and I feel like I been running' all day nonstop, but I gotta pie of that fish 2,500 cash not too bad for one day of work, but I got to get Show his cash to make this mission complete.

By the time I made it out the Northeast, it was after 12:00 am. I parked at the corner of Show block and called his phone so he could send somebody out to meet me and make sure I wasn't followed. When I walked in the door he was sitting' with what looked, to me to be some heavy hitters He introduced me as his cousin, they all showed me love, and it felt good. I asked Show did he want to do business right there, he said Yeah it's all family in here so I handed him the sack with the fifty sacks in it, he looked but didn't even count, offered me a cigar and told me to have a seat. I sat down but didn't say a word. I just listened to these dudes talk big money, who owe, who was doing their job, and what needed to be done. (These motherfuckers for real) So I hear them talking' about South Philly and Dame Name came up. They saying that he was once part of their team, but decided he wanted to be on his own and the fact is that he knew too much and is known for running with them West Philly stick up boys. They didn't trust him and felt he needed to go! (I'm like damn) Now Showboat knows I deal with dame and can get next to him easy, he says...

SHOWBOAT: Red! What you need to take care of this problem for us? I didn't answer, and then one of the other dudes sitting there said "I'm offering half a million for his head, are you in?" I look at Show to make sure this wasn't a test, the look that he gave me was (this shit real) I said let me think on it and I'll let you know for sure tomorrow. They all collectively agreed.

Showboat pulled me to the side and gave me an envelope.

SHOW: Six pies in one day, a hell of a good job my dude, this is for you. If you are smart like I know you are come on board and handle that for us and let's get this money! Its five stacks in the envelope for your troubles. Get at me first thing in the morning. We need that answer.

I left Show house feeling' a little confused and unsure. Dame cool, but is he worth a half a mill to me? I'm really thinking he's not. When I got back to the car I realized I had thirty stacks on me and a brick of coke in the cut that I came up on and never came out of my pocket once. Fucking' with Showboat and his team is paying off real well! I'm really considering putting Dame down!

It's like 9:00am I'm laying' in the bed finally getting some rest when my phone rang.

RED: Who is this?

(On the other end)…

LIL KEY: It's me UNC! You sleep?

RED: Shit, I was what's up?

LIL KEY: You know the black van hit the block last night. They jumped out on us and took everything. They saying' tell the bul Pete come to the front or they will be back, cuz this shit corny. I'm tired of this fucking dudes man.

RED: Let me get up, get myself together and I'll be down there.

CHAPTER 3

SWEET REVENGE

I got on the block around 12:00pm everybody sitting around looking dumb. I asked who was out there when the shit went down.

Lil KEY: Man I was sitting rite there I seen the black van ride by, I stood up to get my burner but before I made it up the block they swung the corner with the side door open before the van stopped they started jumping out, burners drawn. Two went this way, two went that way! Yo, they laid everybody on the ground, like ten motherfuckas, After they robbed us these pussies stuck around talking shit about PETE said tell them they're on his top,.

PETE: Shit I was still at RAY spot smoking n joking "DAMN"

RED: Nobody had their gun on them? REAL FUCKIN SMART...

PETE: I ain't going no-where if they want me tell them come fuckin get me and I stay strapped "KNOW THAT"

RED: Well we out here tonight all of ya'll need to stay on point; I'm not taking no more loses! I got shit to do, I'll be back later!! We talked a few more minutes then I slide off.

I called SHOWBOAT around 2:00pm to let him know I decided to handle that DAME situation. Now they're supposed to give me half up front and the rest when the job is done. I was on my way to meet with Show right hand man and pick up this money, on my way down Roosevelt Blvd. I stopped at the gas station at the corner of Adam's Ave. When I saw that same blue Magnum wagon inside was Lil Dirt Lid and guess who?? Yup!! Dame! Their sitting' in the parking' lot laughing', talking' shit, just having' a good old' time, being as though they didn't see me I just laid my seat back and watched. I'm guessing' that their telling' Dame about last night. I knew this dude was part of this bullshit and I know by now he told them who I was. I just slowly pulled out of the gas stations lot and continued down the Blvd. I'll get gas further down the road.

I met up with Show People. I told him what was going' down and what I just saw. He then began to tell me how they been watching Dame since he left their team and how he's been behind setting up at least fifty percent of the motherfuckas that The west Philly stick up boys were running down on (slimy motherfuckas) now I don't feel bad about what I was about to do.

He gave me the money and we went our separate ways.

Now I'm riding around quarter million on me, burner on my lap, feeling like that bul! Man I look through the rearview and I see the black van like three cars back, they switch lanes, I speed up, Yeah these motherfuckas speed up. Now I'm sure it's them and the only motherfucka could of put the on me was DAME. They were following SHOWBOAT main man in the process they see me talking to him, DAME told these dumb ass dickheads I sold him three brick and I had like twenty pie's in the cut or some bullshit; now while I'm planning and debating about putting DAME down, he already lined me up(THIS SHIT CRAZY) I'm thinking my next move better be my best move, I read the blitz now I'm on their ass, their like two cars back opposite lane, I slowed down actin like I don't see them, I rolled the passenger side windows all the way down, I let them slide up, even though the windows were blacked out I could still see three in the back and the driver no front seat passenger! We side by side now, it's like we're the only two cars on the road, RED look around, raised the burner and opened fire hitting the driver like two or three times then threw like five shots at the back of the van, mashed out! As I look thru the rearview I could see the black van veer off the road hop the curb smash in to the tag and title place at raising sun and the Blvd. I kept it moving!

Now I'm headed back Summerville to tell RAY and PETE what the fuck just happened, when I got to Price St. I parked in the drive way in case somebody followed or got my plate. I walked on the block RAY, PETE and Lil KEY were chilling in front on the spot, I told them what happened. YO! These motherfuckas was hype

PETE: That's what the fuck them coward ass niggas get, I hope you hit'em all

RAY: Yo, RED I think you should go in the crib and fall back until you know what's really good bro!!

Lil KEY sitting there looking scared to death so we went in the spot to smoke and chill for a minute, watch TV Like an hour later the news came on, the top story was an unidentified man was shot and killed on the Blvd. they show the bul TOMMY picture and another passenger was wounded and in critical condition but expected to live they showed the bul DAME picture. I looked at RAY, RAY looked at PETE but nobody said a word. I'm thinking to myself, damn this dude DAME been riding around with these little pussies lining motherfuckas up, he just made my mission so much more easy for me, I wanted to call SHOWBOAT and let him know I'm on the job but decided to wait until I was alone!

We sat talking shit like nothing happened "shit real" you got to lock that shit out your mind convince yourself it never took place, so if they do come asking questions, harassing you talking shit you got a head start (FUCK THESE COPS) I DON'T KNOW SHIT!!

"Knock, knock" Somebody was at the door, I sent Lil KEY to see who it was, he came back smiling;

RED: what the fuck you smiling for?
Lil KEY: Come see for yourself!

I got up went to the door it was STACY and her squad (DAMN) I opened the door and it was ass everywhere, they came in the crib half naked. STACY: Where the fucking ballers at? You can tell when a motherfucka getting that money, what's good?

PETE: Shit you getting all the money, let me hold something, and I see you got your team on deck, Yeah ya'll eating.
STACY: What nigga I'm broke (flashing a hand full of diamonds) don't believe everything you hear
PETE: Yea whatever' (laughing)

STACY told her girls to keep my boys company while we go upstairs and talk, I tapped RAY on the leg and told him; keep his eye on these little bitches –trust no one-.

RAY: I was on that from the door, I got you.

Me and STACY went upstairs

RED: What's good/ what brings you to the hood?
STACY: What? This my hood! But no I'm almost done with that, ima need another one a.s.a.p.
RED: Damn, girl what was that like two days? STACY just smiled and did a little dance
STACY: You should let me put something on the block,
RED: Now why the hell would I do some shit like that? It's already too many motherfuckas trying to put their own shit on the block (CUT IT OUT)

she didn't say nothing, I told her I'd have that for her later that night. She asked if I could bring it to the club, I said no problem… Me and STACY stayed upstairs for a few, let's say "TALKIN" I heard music playing downstairs, when I got down there they were wilding out Lil KEY in the corner getting a "chewy" RAY over here getting a lap dance on my couch, the other two or three chicks stripped naked dancing around in the living room, I just stood there looking

STACY: I know you bitches better be getting paid, that's all I know (laughing).

This went on for about a half hour or so, the little chick KEY had sucking his dick finished up the job, she ask me did I hear about TOMMY and the bul DAME? I looked at her like she was crazy before I said no!! What happened? She goes on to say, he was with them West Philly dude's I guess they're trying to rob something and somebody shot up the black van they be in, shit TOMMY took two to the head and DAME got hit in the chest but I think he's still alive!! I'm like who did that shit? (As if I didn't know) she hunched her shoulders and said, I don't know but that's fucked up though. I agreed! We talked about it for a few more minutes while they got dressed now I'm wondering where PETE went, I walked in the kitchen he got this little bitch on my stove fucking the shit out of her, they both looked back at me but didn't stop, I just laughed and told him to hurry up so they can leave. About twenty minutes pasted they both came out the kitchen sweating like crazy, we all busted out laughing. After STACY and her squad left I went back upstairs to call SHOW, he answered the phone on the first ring,

SHOW: What's good my nigga?

RED: Ain't shit another day at the office, did you hear about the bul?

SHOW: Yeah I heard, that shit crazy

RED: But anyway, I need to grab one more of them things got somebody waiting

SHOW: No doubt, I'm in A.C right now I'll be back around 8:00 I am going to hit your phone when I touch Philly

RED: ok cuz, I'm waiting on you

SHOW: Say no more

I hung up the phone and went back downstairs, these dudes still hype over them little hookas. Look ima need ya'll to knock this shit off so we can make this next move, how much we got left? LIL KEY: I'm done I got five stacks at my spot for you, RAY & PETE both said they need a little more time to finish

PETE: Yo you know them motherfuckas gone be on their shit, I say we go take this shit to them why wait for them to come at us?

RAY: Yo that's what we want, let them come thinking its sweet, we gone act like we don't know what's going on. You go ahead get your grind on, ima play the cut and watch your back, if those pussies come thru the block I'm laying everything down (MY WORD)

I had money on the streets and business to handle, so I told them to hold it down and watch their bodies. I switched burners with Lil KEY and headed out the door, when I hit the block motherfuckas were everywhere word about TOMMY and DAME was traveling fast, the bul DAME had a lot of work on the streets from South Philly to UPT so now I guess dudes fill that DAME is out the game for a minute they come up they out here hustling hard..

It's almost 8:00 so I'm waiting on SHOW call, I drove to the Chinese Buffet on Cotman Ave. to get something to eat and to be close by when that call came thru, need that work.

I'm sitting there eating like a monster, I got all type of food on my table (Shit I paid for it) people looking, I'm going in! It's like 8:15 my phone ring I got food all over my hands by the Time I got myself together it stopped ringing, I called back it was SHOW on the other end but I didn't recognize the number

SHOW: What's good?
RED: I'm on ice waiting on you
SHOW: Meet me at the spot
RED: The spot or the SPOT?
SHOW: (Laughing) the SPOT!!

I finished my food and drank my juice, sat for about five, ten minutes, hit the bathroom then headed out the door.

Man soon as I walked outside I knew something' wasn't right. From across the lot I could see this all white van with black limo tint. The lights out, but I can see steam coming from the tailpipe. I can see at least two heads moving around inside. I walked slowly across the lot to my car. I called Ray phone to let them know what's bout to go down! I chruped my car alarm unlocked the door, popped the trunk, grabbed my burner, and stood there for a few seconds on the phone. I told Ray that I needed him. Lil Key and Pete to meet me at Wyoming and the BLVD I hung up the phone and got in the car and pulled off. Just like I knew the lights on the white van came on and they were coming fast.

I'm trying to figure out how these little fucking bastards keep popping up on me but I know one thing this shit getting corny. I jumped on the Blvd out 5th street their following me like I don't see they ass. I called Ray to see where they were at he answered on the first ring.

Ray: Yo my nigga we here, where you at?
Red: I'm about to turn the corner, these motherfuckers right
    behind me. When I pull up, Wait until I pull over.
Ray: I'm on it (Copy)

When I turned on the Blvd, I slow down, the white van slowed down. I can see Ray, Pete, and somebody else that look like Lil KEY on the side of the road. I know these stickup boys (dickheads) flaming, every time the fuck with my team shit don't work out too good for them. They already got they boy put down and they nut-ass leader laying in the fucking I.C.U. Well shit, here we go again.

When I pulled pass Ray and them on the side of the road I turned my lights out and pulled over. The van stopped, sat for a second, (They confused) then the side door slides open, like three of them' in hoodies and masks jumped out and slowly started walking towards my wheel. I stuck my arm out the window before I could let off a shot Ray came from behind the car and ambushed these assholes. He opened up, Pete had two four pounds letting that shit ring, they busting back bullets flying everywhere the driver tried to peel off, shit Lil Key, Swiss cheesed the van he had an old Tech nine: he had that thing for years and it never jammed. They call there self-running down on me, they laid out like speed bumps in the street.

Ray got hit in the leg. Pete and Lil Key helped him to his car. I just turned my lights on as I slide down the road.

The fact that these motherfuckers done robbed everybody in the city it's no telling who finally caught that ass (Real Shit). I called Ray phone to make sure they were good, he answered like he was in pain but he said it went in and out no big deal. I told them' to go lay low and get at me later!

By the time I got to Broad and Wyoming it was Police, fire engines, ambulances, helicopters; shit went crazy. I kept driving in the opposite direction.

CHAPTER 4

FOCUS ON THE MONEY

Philly: You never know what to expect from one day to the next! Today the next person getting rocked tomorrow it could be me.

The differences between them and me I got a plan, what you think I am running around here for nothing? I put away a nice piece of money, sitting on these two pies until shit is right! See I got this spot o.t it's a gold mine. Soon as I collect the rest of this bread off the streets make sure my Lil team straight I'm in the wind. I had plans on going, setting up shop then bringing Pete and Ray out with me, Lil Key too if he gone fly straight. (I got my eye on him).

It's been about two three months since that situation with the bull Dame and those WP dudes. I been laying low, getting this money. I haven't seen Ray or Lil Key in a few weeks, me and Pete riding. I heard Ray was up and out again. The bullet went in and out his thigh, he good. Word is the bull Dame back out here doing his thing a lot of dudes fucked his money up while he was away so I guess he on some major get back. Little does he know His days numbered he's worth way more dead than alive to me, and after all of this snake ass shit.

Me and Pete slide up on Ray at his mother house to see what was good. When we pulled up he was sitting on the porch with some chick smoking a Dutch of that O.G Kush (You could smell it up the block) at first he didn't see us, then he looked up.

Ray: Ok, my motherfuckin boys on deck.

Red: What it do gunshot?

Ray: Ain't shit, chilling (Laughing)

Pete: When the last time you seen Lil Key?

Ray gave a funny look

Ray: Man, I heard the bul Key getting money with Dame and them now.

Red: What? He was doing what?

Ray: Yo! I saw them on the block and in the club together ain't no way he up under them dudes if he ain't eating or running his fucking mouth.

Red: Yo, get him on the phone!

Ray tried calling Lil Key phone like five times or more no answer. We sat on his mom's porch for like an hour.

Ray: Red I need some work! I'm back on my bullshit. I need to get back on the block.

Red: Alright I got you covered like a blanket, how much you working wit?

Ray: Shit not much.

If I buy an onion I need you to throw me one.

Red: ARD, I got you.

Me and Pete hop back in the car, we out here chasing this money. I had money on the block and like five other spots all at once. (I can't complain) At this point I just want to tie up loose ends, stack the rest of this money up and get low. But we all know that sounds too easy. On the way to the money we ran into a little situation! Stacy called my phone talking crazy. She said he said that I said some shit. I supposed to have set her up.

Stacy: Red we know each other a long time and I know you ain't have them bitch-ass niggas run in my crib man! (Snappin) I fucking know you not that stupid so RED I'm going to ask you. Did you have your hands in that?

Red: What the fuck are you talking about? Why the fuck you calling me with this shit? If somebody crossed you we can deal with that but don't ever call my phone on any punk shit like that. Now how the fuck did my name get in this shit?

Pete: In what shit?

Stacy: Fuck that shit, somebody ran up in the crib, took all my shit (upset) they tied up two of my girls and my nephew, tore my house the fuck up!

Red: So why you come at me for some shit like that? I thought we were good!

Stacy: No! I saw DAME and the young bul KEY the day after it happened, so I stopped to tell them I got robbed them motherfuckers told me I better check with you because you the one running around the city lining people up, getting people robbed in shit!!!

RED: Who? Said what? Yo PETE these motherfuckas' STACY- BABY that diffidently wasn't my work but I

28

guarantee you I will deal with it though... Lay low for a minute- A! YOU AIN'T TALK TO ME!

STACY: OK!! OK!

When I got off the phone with STACY I was on fire inside, I told PETE what these pussies was up to, these motherfuckas want to blame me for their dirt, dudes want to get rid of me but scared to face me rather do some sneaky little bitch shit. But I got something for that ass I better not see LIL KEY or DAME, until I find out what's going on- those two niggas dead in this city!!

PETE and I made a couple more runs before I dropped him off at the spot. I called SHOW to let him know the word on the street and really just to check on him. We agreed to meet at the diner on south street, I made it their first so I sat by the window like I always do I need to see who's coming or going!! SHOWBOUT walked thru the door about twenty minutes later, I watched as he stood outside and used the phone before he Came in (I PEEP EVERYTHING) he walked up and slide in the booth (SMILIN)

SHOW: What it do cuz

RED: Ain't shit what's good?

SHOW: Cuz shit getting crazy, motherfuckas on some real bullshit; these corny-ass dudes ain't got any loyalty. Your young bul outta pocket! YEAH!! You know I see and hear it all

RED: What young bul??

SHOW: The bul KEY he out here actin like a real nut, telling motherfuckas that you a snake I see him riding around wit the bul DAME he got KEY robbing dudes n shit heard they supposed to be coming at me or some shit

I sat there in a daze couldn't believe what I was hearing- I sipped my lemon aid took a deep breath before I spoke

RED: Just have the rest of that money when I get off work and don't worry about KEY or nobody else, SHOW they got me on my bullshit! We sat and talked while I finished my sandwich and my drink; I got up first and walked out the diner. I parked all the way up 5th or 6 St. I looked both ways then started walking. When I got up near the "NET" I decided to hang around for a few do a little shopping, in an hour I managed to spend almost 2,000 on POLO shirts and sneakers (TIME TO GO)

I walked up to my car popped the trunk so I could put my bags in! Out of the corner of my eye, who do I see? YEAH! Fuckin DAME, LIL KEY riding shot gun DIRT in the back seat, traffic on South Street was backed up so they were literally sitting right in my face but never looked over at me. So I played my part stood still until they drove on. I slowly walked around my car and got in, hoping they didn't come to chill but just sliding threw, I pulled out the parking spot making sure their like 5 or 6 cars ahead of me, they chilling music blasting (LAUNCHIN) they never even saw me!!

They turned off South Street and drove deeper into South Philly, I continued to follow. I called PETE to let him know where I was and what was going on. PETE said I wasn't far, and he was on his way. By that time we were crossing Washington Ave. and 8th St. it's only one car between us they slowed down so I pulled over and laid my seat back. They pulled over on Washington Ave. all three of them got out the car, just sat and watched, they're all laughing and smoking enjoying life. A few minutes later DAME and DIRT shook Lil KEY hand as they got back in the car KEY stood there and talked to them for a second from outside the car then they pulled off (IM LIKE OH SHIT IT'S ON) Lil KEY hung around finished his cigarette before he started walking. PETE called my phone,

PETE: WHAT'S UP IM AT BROAD AND WASHINGTON! WHERE YOU AT?

RED: I'm on this little nigga ass he walking up 8ᵗʰ right off of Washington go to 8ᵗʰ and Federal and pull over, HURRY UP!!

PETE: Well shit I'm almost there

I'm watching KEY just a strolling, ditty bopping when he got like a half block from Federal PETE texted my phone "IM HERE" so I parked jumped out, grabbed my p-89 and followed on foot YO! He never seen me coming, I walked right up on him he looked like he seen a ghost I never said a word I just smiled and flashed my burner, I could see PETE parked at the corner so I grabbed KEY arm and made him walk with me. I'm hoping he don't resist and make me rock-out broad daylight! His best bet is to just do what I say; he walked with little to no resistance

KEY: RED let me holla at you cuz, I ain't tell them dudes nothing I didn't say a word!!

KEY: Red please cuz I promise I didn't cross you (CRYIN)

When we got to the corner PETE was acting like he was fixing his tire, he had the trunk open and the hazard lights on me and Lil KEY walked up stood and talked like everything was regular. I walked KEY to the trunk pulled the burner told him to get in or I would put him in, crying like a bitch he climbed in the trunk, I shut the trunk walked around got in the passenger seat PETE waited a few seconds jumped in and we were gone!! Pete dropped me off at my car and I followed him to the spot!

CHAPTER 5

SOMEBODY GOTTA DIE...

Duct taped to the chair, I'm upstairs I can hear him screaming for help (CAN'T NOBODY HELP YOU NOW)

"TIME TO TALK"

When I entered the basement the look on KEY face was of guilt and fear, I didn't even look at him, I sat across the room and smoked my Dutch while PETE "Questioned him" when I walked over to him he couldn't look me in the face.

RED: So, you're playing both sides of the fence! What you telling them pussies?

Lil KEY: I ain't told them shit! DAME the one trying to get somebody to rob you!

RED: What pussy (SMACKED HIM WITH THE GUN) you knew this but you didn't say shit? So you down with them! You was gone rob me? Huh? You was gone rob me? I showed you nothing but love, this what I get? No fucking loyalty! See that's the problem with you motherfuckers, but you know what pussy- I hope you

33

were at lease loyal to GOD cause I'm about to send you to meet him!!!

Lil KEY: Wait, WAIT! RED please don't kill me man, I can tell you what's gone down- I can tell you DAME next move, that's why I did that shit so I could get you more info, I promise cuz, my word!

RED: Yeah?? Well you got three minutes to tell me some shit that's worthy my fucking time!

I stood there with my gun in my hand as KEY tried his best to tell me something about somebody to save his bitch made, disloyal ass, snitch ass, life. He went on to tell me about DAME plan to rob me; he also had plans of putting STACY down- let bitch ass KEY tell it!! He say that he heard DAME was calling his out of town hitta, some dude they call NINE FINGER R he supposed to be some major rock out boy, he play with them burners real heavy. All dude known for is taking money and catching bodies! Me personally I don't give a fuck about this dude but I needed to hear the whole story.

Lil KEY: I told you everything FAM, please just let me go,

RED: Yeah! I know you told everything, just like you sat over there telling those pussies all my shit! (SMACKIN HIM) I'm a let you go cuz, may your soul be free!!

Red put the barrel of the gun to the side of KEY head and pulled the trigger, his body jerked as his blood and brains hit the plastic sheet on the floor (EVERYTHING WENT QUIT)

RED: PETE rap this shit up

PETE: (SHAKING HIS HEAD) DONE!!!

We laid low until after dark, carried the body to the car drove down DAME strip, pushed KEY dead body out the moving car. This was to send a message "THIS IS WHAT HAPPENS WHEN YOU CROSS THE BOSS"

The next day I tried to call STACY just to check in and see what's good (NO ANSWER) I tried a few more times, SAME THING, a couple days before I gave STACY some work to help her get back after those bitch ass dudes robbed her, haven't heard from her since! I'm debating should I pop up on her or not.

My phone rang,

RED: Who this?

Other end…
Yo! This SHOW! Cuz this fuckin DAME dude out of control, this motherfucker fucking with my money now! He and his little team of thieves just ran down on one of my boys spots, and he knows who the fuck he is.

RED: Damn claim down cuz
SHOW: Fuck that shit cuz, I heard they telling people you
killed Lil KEY, and I'm hearing they done snatched
Stacy ass up the other day, right up the street from the
strip club on Wyoming
RED: WHAT???
SHOW: Yea cuz I need to meet with you so we can discuss
the real business at hand
RED: JUST TELL ME WHEN AND WHERE

SHOW: meet me tomorrow night in the white room at
    MEZZANINE on price (THE OLD MORGANS)
RED: IM THERE

When I got off the phone with SHOW I decided to slide past STACY spot to see what the fuck was really going on! For some reason soon as I turned on to STACY block I knew shit wasn't right, it was like this funny feeling in my stomach by I keep moving closer. I parked, got out walked up to the door. I could hear music playing; I tried to peep in the window but couldn't see shit! So I banged on the door, waited, banged again, then I tried the door knob, it was open. My hair stood up on the back of my neck. When I walked in I could see that someone was there looking for something in a hurry, furniture thrown around, I walked through looked around then slowly made my way up the steps. When I reached STACY bedroom I pushed the door open (DAMN) I could barely stand to look.

They had my fuckin homie BUTT-NAKED Duct taped laid out on the floor she looked beat up pretty bad, and I can see she was differently raped before they put one single bullet in her face (SUCH A PRETTY FACE) SMH!! It's like I couldn't stop staring at her, I forced myself to walk out, I drove like ten blocks away stop called 911 from a pay phone so they could go get STACY body out of that fuckin house, I got back in the car and keep sliding!

I'm driving around the city collecting this money, all I keep seeing is STACY body laid out on the floor, I just trying to get this cash straight and get low but before I can even think about moving on- I NEED TO PAY DAME A VISIT!!...

CHAPTER 6

I T'S about 9:00pm ME and SHOWBOAT sitting in
MEZZANINE busting it up, I'm old school Whisky
sour, SHOW sipping Grey goose straight

SHOW: They found STACY body; her people gone crazy,
    I think you best get at the bul before STACY brothers
    do! Cuz he got all type people on his top!!
RED: He better pray they get him before me

    Me and SHOW tapped glasses as to say "CHEERS" but
more so to say "BE CAREFUL WATCH YOUR BACK" As
we're sitting there talking SHOWBOUT right hand man
slides in the booth. The bul they call BYGTYME see he was
the one I was in the car with when the cowards was following
us, he made the original order for me to put the bul down,
it was his money they gave me so now I guess they want the
job done.
    The bul BYGTYME he more behind the scene then
front line so I'm wondering what he up to

BYGTYME: Yo cuz what you need some help? You having
    second thoughts or you need me to locate him for you?
    What's good?
RED: Yo SHOW what's up with your mans?

BYGTYME: Cuz this nigga outta control, somebody needs to deal with this shit, if you can't handle that shit let me know so I can put somebody on it that can.

RED: I told you it's done, it's fucking done!!!

Just as fast as he popped up he was gone me and SHOW hung out for a few; I started getting this strange feeling so I decided to slide. The crowed outside in the parking lot across the street from the club was deeper then the one inside! I parked on Germantown Ave. so I walked down the hill; I have a habit of looking over my shoulder whenever I walk alone. By the time I made it to corner of Price & Germantown I noticed one dude slide out the crowed and the fact that he was wearing all black with a hoodie on and everybody else seem to be a little more dressier made him stand out, I keep walking like I didn't peep the blitz I'm trying to make it to my car, my burner is in the trunk (I KNOW IM SLIPPIN) halfway point I looked back to see where he was, this motherfucka gone I looked around but it's like he disappeared! When I got to the car I went straight to the trunk and grabbed my burner stood there for a minute or two before I got in! I drove down to Germantown & Chelten then made an illegal left onto Chelten Ave. I'm checking my rear view I got my burner on my lap I don't know what to think or who the fuck dude was but I know one thing I'm not gone out like no nut, I stopped at a red light at Chew Ave. looking down fucking with the radio I didn't notice the law right behind me I can see the white cop behind the wheel running my plate, when the light turned green I pulled off slow crossed the intersection then pulled over in front of the deli and got out. Two white cops I put my hands in the air as they drove by (FUCKING WITH THEM) they gave me dirty looks and keep driving. I walked in the deli to waste a minute let them cops find somebody else to fuck with, I stayed in the deli no longer then 3-5 minutes turned around and walked back out (WHAT THE FUCK) standing on the corner across the street was this dude in all black wearing a hoodie the same fucking dude from outside the club. My gun is in the car so I tried to play it off and walk the other way, bad idea; here he comes I can see him walking fast rite towards me, I cross the street at Chew & Woodlawn that's when he opened fire. Yo! Bullets were flying and I was trying to get the fuck low, I started running but it seemed like my legs were xtra heavy, then I started feeling short of breath, but I keep running and he keep shooting it all only lasted about a minute or so but to me it was like he'd never stop, I cut in between two cars and it was like something told my body to lay down but my mind still telling me to run let's just say when I woke up they were putting me in the back of an ambulance, I opened my eye and moved my feet to make sure I was alive!

Now while I'm laying up in the fucking hospital shot the fuck up the streets are going crazy DAME out in the open talking like he rule the world now, TY and his nephew DIRT out there searching for my boy PETE he's been hitting my phone like crazy lately (THEY GOT MY BOY SHOOK) STACY people out looking for DAME, if they catch him before I can get right that's my bread out the fucking window. I need to get the fuck outta here this shit here is in the way! I lay up in the hospital for about a week it seemed much longer, the day I was getting discharged SHOWBOAT called my phone telling me how these motherfuckers killed my boy

RAY on his mother's front porch (I CRIED LIKE A LIL GIRL) that was my boy! I told SHOW when I get out I'm coming straight to his spot, game over, it's going down.

I know I told SHOW I would come straight to his spot when I got out but I had to go past RAY people house and be with his family and show my love, when I pulled up I see RAY mom in front of the door with her church group crying and praying, they still had crime scene tape on the porch, it was hard for me to get out the car but I felt I had to! I was in mad pain chewing Percocet like candy I walked up to RAY mother when she saw me she ran to me, she was about to hug me but I guess she could see I was in pain. She touched me on my arm and cried about her boy it hurt my heart to see her like this over some punk shit, she asked me was I okay, I told her I was good the one bullet went straight through my leg the second one hit my shoulder she shook her head and told me to lay low, be careful And leave the streets alone, I told her that was my plan kissed her on the cheek shook RAY little brother hand told him if he ever needs me for anything just hit my phone then I left! On my way to SHOW spot I drove though the hood to see who was out, see if I run into PETE the block was empty, so I drove back TOPSIDE SV to see if he was around, find out what the fuck is up with this TY shit, but he was nowhere to be found so I kept it moving.

I decided that I would look for PETE after I go check SHOW out he was at the (spot) in the hood not far from Summerville when I got to show house cops were everywhere, in and out of SHOW spot all on the block checking in parked car trunks, under cars, in trash cans! I pull over at the corner to watch a few minutes later they brought SHOW out in cuffs (DAMN) the motherfucka DAME put the law on

SHOW and he told the I'm the one that killed Lil KEY so now SHOW booked, I can't find PETE, the law on my top and I'm out here on some real go dumb shit looking for this slime ass dude DAME and I have an idea where he might be.

CHAPTER 7

DEAD MAN WALKIN

When I finally slipped away from all the trigger happy cops on SHOW block I went back to the hotel, tired, long ass day I laid across the bed to rest my eyes before I count this money and wait for SHOW call, if he calls me for bail or whatever it's done. I fell asleep woke up with six missed calls ten missed text messages most of them were from females one from BIGTYME none from PETE! I called BIGTYME back to see what was good, did he hear from SHOW?

BIGTYME: YO RED I'm going to handle that issue now, I need you to fall back and concentrate on the situation at hand! Oh yea I find out where this DAME dude baby mom rest at, I hear he stops in from time to time! You got them boys on your head so play smart I will check you later.

RED: I'm on it, later!

I hung up the phone and laid back down I know I can't go back to sleep cause now my mind is on fast forward, so instead of counting sheep I started counting my money, in the last few months I accumulated about half a million, when I first took on the job to deal with DAME it was all about the money now I lay here thinking I would of killed his ass for free!

I finally got my ass up and took a shower I called back the rest of the numbers on my missed call last, the little chick KIM blowing my phone up, she text me "WYD" COME GET ME! So I called her

KIM: Hello
RED: What it do?
KIM: I thought u were coming to get me
RED: NAW
KIM: WHAT? WHY NOT?
RED: You can come to me, I'm at the telly
KIM: Oh really? I'm on my way
RED: CALL WHEN YOU GET DOWNSTAIRS
KIM: What room is it?
RED: CALL WHEN YOU GET DOWNSTAIRS!!!
KIM: DAMMNNN, OK, OK

See KIM this little bad jawn I meant out partying one night got her number been trying to hit since, now she chasing me (Cocked burner) I know I have shit to do but I'm about to tear her little ass up, I been trying to fuck her for a minute now and she throwing that shit at me! I rolled that good Kush popped a couple perks and awaited her arrival.

She called from the parking lot downstairs (I'm hype) I went down to meet her cause I didn't want to give her the room number, we walked in the room, she took off that coat DAMN ass phat, my dick was instantly rock hard. I lit the

Dutch bull shitted for a few, she went right in sucked my dick so good I was dizzy, she wanted me to slide in without a hat I was like pause. So she grabbed the condom started sucking again stopped grabbed her phone said she had to use the bathroom got up walked to the door stopped then went in the bathroom! Ain't nothing slow about me, I get up right behind her walk to the door lock it back walk back to the bed grab my burner and wait for her to come out, she came out holding her phone still trying to play sexy. I flashed the burner in her face, she about to scream, I told her to shut the fuck up and sit down, she sat down looking scared to death, I didn't say a word just held the gun on her and watching the door sixty seconds later I know it somebody tried to open the door, I put the burner against her head and my finger over my lips (sshhh) she didn't move. I could see the shadow under the door they tried to open it again waited then slowly walked away, I waited a second then got up, made sure nobody was out there then walked back over to KIM if that's her name.

RED: Ok, that was cute but you got like three minutes to tell me what's going the fuck on before I blow your fucking pretty little face off!

At first she couldn't speak, she looked at me and said

KIM: I don't know what's going on (Start crying)
RED: Bitch game time done, fuck that crying tell me who sent you, WHO THE FUCK SENT YOU?

She played dumb, said she had no idea, she said she was there cause she was digging me, this bitch think I'm slow. Until I took her phone, oh she know she was fucked I can see it in her face. I went thru recent calls first name, last call "MY BABY D" so I call DAME answer

DAME: Damn T what happened?

I didn't say a word just hung up and turned to face T

RED: So they sent you to line me up? That's fucked up, I liked you!

KIM-T: I'M SORRY HE MADE ME DO IT; HE SAID HE WAS GOING TO KILL ME; I'LL DO ANYTHING, PLEASE!!

RED: You can start by finishing what you started. As I pushed towards her face, she looked at my dick like as if she would try and bite it so I gripped up tight on my gun

KIM-T: OK I'LL DO IT REAL GOOD, PROMISE YOU WON'T KILL ME

RED: I PROMISE! (SMORK)

She handled her business sucking like it was the last dick she would ever suck little did she know it was. I busted all in her face she looked up at me then I shot her! Knowing she called and texted my phone I had to do something quick and slide out, so I texted her phone cussing her out for standing me up, "I said I waited you never showed I left" "call me when you done playing. I wiped the phone clean put it in her bag, wrapped her the bag and anything else she had with her up in the sheet then in the blanket, I waited, good thing she was small I rolled her out to my car on the luggage cart, put her ass in the trunk and was gone!! Being as though the car was rented off of a credit card of a person I don't know, I took the car up Cobb's Creek and torched the whole thing (FUCK IT)

They let SHOW out on $100,000 bail on a bunch of bullshit trumped up charges I didn't want to call him until this shit is done! I drove to the address that BIGTYME gave me on DAME baby mom, I sat across the street and just watched I can see people moving around in the house but had no way of knowing who was in there so I sat and sat, I'm not leaving until I get what I come for! About an hour pasted and somebody finally came out the door, it's a female, she looks like the description BIGTYME gave me of the BM so I followed behind in the truck to see where she was going and if she was going to meet DAME. She walked a few blocks then dipped in a corner store, I pulled over and waited, she was in the store for about fifteen minutes I was just about to get out the car and see what was going on when this black tinted out crown Vic pull up, I let my seat back so I can get a good look but not be seen, the door opened and who stepped out Yup!! DAME, he went to the trunk and got this large sneaker bag, it looked like whatever was in there was heavy I was so hype I almost jumped out and went at him right there, but this look like it could get fun and maybe I can come up off this asshole before I down him so I decided to chill watch it play out!

DAME walked in the corner store with this cocky swag, he feeling like the king of PHILLY right now he stayed in the store for about ten minutes I guess making a drop and talking shit. The store door opened and the BM came out carrying the sneaker bag, she looked around like she was nerves before walking back the way she came! I sat and waited DAME came out the store stood there a few seconds then diddy-booped back to his car, I laughed to myself let him pull off first then hided toward BM spot (I want what's in that bag)

When I turned the corner she was walking down the street looking straight ahead, I drove past her, pulled over trying to decide should I grab her off the street or wait until she make it to her destination? I think I'll wait because it might be more already there! I noticed she's headed back to her spot where I followed her from to start so I drove a block away from her crib got out and posted up! I could see her walking down the block I hide behind a few trash cans on her porch, I pulled my gun took it off safety and waited. I don't know who else is in the house but at this point I really don't care. She walked up on the steps singing I guess she was happy she made it home safe or so she thought I waited until I heard the key slide in the lock before I pounced on her ass, I jumped out and put burner in her face

RED: Open the fucking door bitch and don't you dare scream

BM/EBONY: What the fuck FAM? You got the wrong one, who you looking for?

RED: Bitch if you don't open this fucking door they gone be looking for your head (GRABBING THE BAG OUT OF HER HAND) let me get that

BM/EBONY: Here take the bag and go ahead!!

RED: (SMACKING HER WITH THE GUN) Bitch open that shit now

When she pushed the door open all I could smell was weed so I held her in front of me, sat the bag by the front door, shut the door, I took her with me to search the house! In and out every room, under every bed, nobody

RED: Listen! If you tell me where the rest of the shit is I won't kill you.

She didn't hesitate to take me to the middle room closet and begin to hand me stacks and stacks of cash at least a hundred thousand

BM/EBONY: Fuck this shit take it, just take it (CRYING) I'm not dying over this shit fuck DAME that pussy don't care about me he keep me in some dumb shit, take it, please just take it and go!!!

I started stuffing the money in the bag I don't even know what's in the other bag I would have to assume that it was coke I turned to her on the floor crying

RED: Tell DAME, RED said this will do for now come to the front or I will be back. Be thankful I didn't kill you.

I grabbed the bags, blow her a kiss, opened the door and slide out, I walked fast to my truck put the bags in the back and headed to the spot after the little bitch KIM – T or who the hell ever, I don't stay at hotels in the city so I've been staying over the bridge in the cut, I figured once I make it in, count this money, I will call and see what's up with SHOW then I can finally get some rest.

CHAPTER 8

I woke up around 12:00 the next day damn I needed to be up and out by 10:00 am. I fell to sleep before I could call and check on SHOW but I did get to count this money and get some sleep I jumped in the shower and got dressed with in an hour. I hit the street with one thing on my mind, get this money including the rest of my bread off that bitch nigga head that situation with his BM should bring him to the front I had him if I wanted but I needed that cash first! Oh he going to slip again and when he does I'll be right there.

It's like as soon as I stepped out the door my phone went crazy I mean I had calls from motherfuckers I haven't seen or heard from in a minute! Dudes talking about they need work, I got motherfuckers calling me about STACY, and I got that call from SHOW telling me he was good and a bunch of random bullshit but not one call from or about PETE. I drove past his mom house to see if his car was out on her block but it wasn't so I stopped and ask his little brother MEEK have he seen him.

His brother saying he hasn't heard from him in weeks, this shit getting crazy. I got too much on my mind so I'm driving aimlessly around the city (my phone ring)

RED: WHO THIS??

No answer! So I said it again

RED: YO! WHO THIS??
DAME: IT'S ME MOTHERFUCKER

I paused for a second.

RED: PUSSY WHY THE FUCK U CALLING MY PHONE (NUTASS DUDE)
DAME: WHAT?? YOU DICKHEAD YOU REALLY THINK THAT SHIT SWEET LIKE THAT HUH?? YOU PUT YOUR HANDS ON MY BABYMOMS NIGGA?
RED: DIG THIS, FUCK YOU! WHERE YOU AT?
DAME: OH I SEE YOU THINK I'M PLAYING, I GOT YOUR BOY!!
RED: WHAT PUSSY??
DAME: YEAH! I GOT YOUR FUCKING SOILDER, WELL WHAT'S LEFT OF HIM YOU WANT HIM? IF SO YOU NEED TO BE FINDING A WAY TO GET MY FUCKING MONEY AND MY WORK THAT YOU TOOK AND PUT TEN MORE ON THERE FOR TOUCHING MY BITCH..
RED: OK SO YOU REALLY ARE FUCKING CRAZY HUH?? BUT YOU RITE WHEN AND WHERE BOSS??
DAME: UPTOWN! BEHIND KING HIGH SCHOOL AT 7:00
RED: YUP!! I'M THERE. YO HE BETTER BE OK OR
DAME: OR WHAT MOTHERFUCKER, DON'T FUCKING PLAY WITH ME TOMORROW 7:00

He hung up, I sat there on the side of the road mad as a motherfucker I knew PETE had to be slipping to let these dumbasses snatch him up, it's know way I'm giving this money back what I am going to do is show up at 6:00 set up on this dickhead all he doing is making it easier for me, he think he bringing me to the front but he's about to get cashed in!!

So now I'm riding around with my "head cut off" trying to figure out how in the hell am I going to pull this shit off, I had money to pick up from three different sections of the city I need to focus but this shit got me tripping! I went uptown first (back eastside) to check my folks make sure shit was straight then I headed down HP 8th and pike I got a goon squad out there getting that bread. Then I had to hit WP (52ND N Market) by the time I was done running around it was like 1:00a.m but I still couldn't sit still. I drove through South Philly to see who was out but it was like a dessert, nobody in sight! I went in the house around 3-4a.m I finally laid across the bed at about 5a.m and tried to rest.

I woke up to the sound of a fucking jackhammer I was about to snap then I realized it was 2:00p.m, I got my ass up knowing I was in for a hell of a day. I had four hours before I learn the fate of my right hand man, all I could think about was that day in the park the young bull was talking real reckless I heard this motherfucker say he was going to kill PETE so no matter how this shit play out that little motherfucker got to go. I sat around the house until 5p.m thinking of a master plan, I figure I'd show up at 6p.m play the cut and watch give myself a head start, see what's my best move. I didn't tell anyone about the meeting I just need my boy to come out of this alive.

I got to the park at like 6:10 sat in the woods and waited, I seen two black SUV'S pull to the back of the high school and just sat there it was like ten minutes till 7. When I saw them (two dudes) Carrie something rolled up in a white sheet, (damn I know that's my homie) I couldn't move, sat there staring. I finally broke away and got the fuck out of dodge. I'll catch DAME ass later.

CHAPTER 9

FED UP

I got a tip from my little soldier, he informed me that this dude DAME hanging out in the barber shop on 24th street in SP so I decided to pay him a visit. When I got to the shop I had fire in my eyes I walked straight in, DAME sitting there, the bull DIRT in there with him MAL the Baber goes for his gun but I was on him I put the burner to his head like let me get that, turned and aimed it at DAME

DAME: WHAT'S THIS SHIT ABOUT?

RED: YEA? YOU STUPID? YOU KNOW WHAT THE FUCK THIS ABOUT! SO YOU JUST KILLED HIM ANYWAY HUH?

DIRT: FUCK YOU COME IN HERE LIKE YOU THE FUCKING MOB PUSSY!

RED: (DIDN'T SAY A WORD) SHOT HIS ASS.... FUCK YOU

DAME: DAMN

RED: WHEN I COME BACK DAME IT'S FOR YOUR ASS

I backed out the door with both burners raised, and was gone!

Now PETE dead, KEY, STACY! BYGTYME still on my ass, he's asking for his money back if I don't get it done.

I had dude more than one time but don't just want to kill his ass he got to pay (literally) for all this bullshit, I kill him and somebody else get all that bread and coke? FUCK THAT!! I want him on my terms.

I haven't heard a word or seen Dame and his boys since the day at the barber shop! I've really been thinking of getting out of town for a while, I can't believe they killed Pete like that he was the only one I could half trust and now he's gone, smfh...

I set at the edge of the bed feeling sorry for myself for about an hour before I snapped myself out of it I can't help but blame myself for Pete's death, but I got moves to make and sitting around ain't gone get it done. I decided to take a ride through SP and see if I run across this fucking Dame dude or any of them, they killed Pete I'm not gone just let it go down like that this here is war you kill one of mine I kill two of yours...

I'm riding around South Philly it's like 11:30PM and not a soul in sight I bang a left on to 22nd St. up near Southside pizza and pulled over and parked. Only thing that was popping was the Chinese store a couple dudes were out front selling loud and losies I let my seat back rolled up and took in the sights, I sat for about an hour or so at first nothing was moving but as soon as I was about to call it a night guess who the fuck walks in the store? "DIRT" Dame little flunky that I shoot in the leg at the barber shop! (GOT EM) he was the main one talking about killing Pete over that shit wit his uncle TY, I set and watched his whole play, he went in ordered food cop some losies from dude outside the store, stood there smoking and joking while he wait on his food I'm looking him right in the face and he don't even see me.

When he went back in the store for his food, I started the engine he came out and started to walk down point breeze toward Morris St. I slowly pulled off behind him he never seen me coming soon as he turned to go through the lot at the corner of Morris I pulled up and popped out like what's good? The look on his face was priceless he couldn't believe his eyes.

RED: Yea long time no see

DIRT: Cuz listen I'm out of that shit, I don't even fuck wit Dame like that no more, get that gun out my face

RED: You really should of never fucked wit that clown to begin wit and maybe you'd still be alive and pulled the trigger twice stood over his body, this one for Pete and shoot again! It was as if everything had went in slow motion for a few then reality set in, I tossed the gun on the front seat jump in my truck and was gone!

CHAPTER 10

EITHER ME OR YOU

It's 2 AM I'm finally trying to get some rest when the phone goes crazy it's Bygtyme telling me the feds just ran all up in both of his spots found all kind of shit, he saying that he needs to leave town and if I were smart I would too he also said he want that bread he put up back if Dame not dealt wit within the next few days before he roll out, I told him they'll be no refunds but the job will be completed, he hung up..

I know one thing for sure I've been doing me, living life, staying in hotels, renting cars, tricking, flipping that work, having it my way, I've been stacking my bread but I'm not about to give this bread back. In fact I need to get DAME out of here so I can get the rest of mine and get low before Bygtyme try and disappear.

For the next day or two my mission was strictly Dame and Dame only, I'm all over the city looking for dude, he's nowhere to be found, I'm riding around angry and confused thinking about all the shit that just went down, all I lost dealing wit these fucking Philly streets I'm really all alone in this shit now my whole team dead or locked the fuck up I need to get this over wit! I've been driving around for hours, I went past every spot that I can think this dude might be. I even went past his baby mom house "YEA" the same baby mom I ran down on and robbed, she was more than happy to tell me his whereabouts she said he beat her ass and stopped fucking wit her and their son after that shit went down, she said he staying in Southwest wit same chick taking care of her kids, she put me straight on his top gave me the address and all. I guess she could see it in my face because she offered a hug told me if I need anything to holla at her I took the info and kept it moving.

Now we on to something, I went and sat on the address in SW for a whole day and nothing but I'm patient, I already decided that I'm not going anywhere until I deal wit this bullshit so. Now I see kids playing on the porch, I'm not killing any kids! So I wait and wait no Dame I'm starting to think that bitch was lien as soon as I was about to leave I see this white Jeep parking in front of the address so I wait, lay back and I'll be damn there his is (I SEE YOU) he goes in the trunk bring in the groceries hug the kids on the porch as he go inside (I GOT YOU) now I know what he's driving and where he lay his head. I stayed outside that house all night this motherfucka probably in there eating dinner or laid up fucking! Well he better enjoy because it might be his last.

Its 6:30am I haven't moved an inch, I can't. All I can think of is Stacy laying there naked dead and Pete wrapped up dead in the park and Key damn LIL Key I feel responsible for it all, everything was running smooth until this asshole decided to make me the mark, he used to be my homie, that's how that Philly life be you never know who waiting for you to slip, it could be your day one been plotting since day one.

Around 7:30 I see the front door open, Dame and some chick hugged up playing kissy face (HOW CUTE) Dame walked down the steps looking around as if he could feel me watching, he triple checked before he got in the Jeep, he started it up and set there for a minute, I started my engine and just waited! I wanted to run up on the Jeep and light his ass up but to many people around so I'll wait for him to make his next move.

He finally pulled off, I had to make a U-turn rite quick and get behind him and hope he don't see me, I stayed back but close enough to keep him in sight from the looks of things he's headed to South Philly at this point it don't matter one of us gone die today! He pulled into the gas station on Broad and Wharton I pulled over on Broad Street and watched he gassed up his Jeep talked on the phone for a few minutes and pulled back on Broad so I pulled back behind him!

Seems like I've been tailing this dude all day I want to get all the bread I can out of this dude before I dead his ass, I know he got to stop at one of his money holes, pick up spot so far he just on some ride around the city shit! I could of off him ten times by now but I know he got some money and I need that!

He turned down this little block Wilder St. pulled over in got out, I double parked and dropped my lights I need to see what he's doing. He went in the trunk pulled out a big black plastic bag the way he keep looking around let me know something in that bag that I want, Dame hollered up to the window and couple dudes came to the door I couldn't recognize them from where I set but they're all the same to me (FUCK EM) Dame looked over his shoulder one last time before he took the bag in the house, I hurry up and parked got out pulled my hood up over my head and played the cut, while I'm waiting and watching I see this all blacked out magnum wagon pull up some fat bul jumped out went in the back and came out wit a big black plastic bag hollered up to the window and the young bul come to the door! Ok then let's play! The dude in the black wagon came dropped off and left Dame still in there.

Close to an hour past, finally Dame came out the door looked around got in his Jeep and left but I didn't follow, naw I got another plan, I slowly walked up to the house hollered up to the window and BOOM the front door swing open, I pull my gun and go in! The way I see it I'm too far in to turn back so it's all out.

When I stepped through the door it was the mother load I guess this is their safe house where they count and breakdown the young buls inside couldn't be no more than 20 and the other one was like 17 I got the drop on them they seem more surprised at the fact I had the balls to pop in on my own, by myself I didn't ask no questions or waste any time' I made them both get face down, I didn't want to kill them if I didn't have to. I tied both of them up grabbed one of the empty black trash bags off the floor and started filling it up, listen it had to be at least 50,000 easy not including the work, I put all that shit in the bag before I walked out I said "Tell Dame Red said HI" and I was gone!

That's nothing compared to what he took from me but every score count, I'm hoping he have more for more to get before I out him, when I get where ever it is I'm going I need to be straight, fall back for a minute then set up shop O T once I get this other quarter mill from Bygtyme for Dame head, do the math, I'm good I can go anywhere I want do anything I want, start life over, a new beginning. But only one thing standing in my way "Dame" well not for long

CHAPTER 11
SLOW AND EASY

I've been trying to lay low after that last episode but I can't sit still, I know Dame out here getting money and it's making me crazy I can't sleep, all I can think of is getting as far away from here as possible not for good, just long enough to let shit air out, don't get me wrong I love Philly but if you play in these streets you better follow the rules of the game and rule #1 you don't cross family, Dame one of them people that don't follow rules so he must get out the game.

So now that I know where dude rest his head "I'm around" I've been following this dude for two days I think he's on to me because he ain't made any more drops or pickups I got him under pressure all he do is drive around looking though his rear view mirror, I'm tired of playing now, whatever money I didn't get from him, I won't get from him, next time I catch him slipping, where ever I catch him slipping, I'm leaving him there…

I've been hanging around all day, up and down the block no sign of Dame I think he figured out where I picked up his tail at, he haven't been back here I'm about to run up in that damn house and see who the fuck inside but I know those kids in there and I doubt that there's any money in there so imma play the street he'll pop up again for now I'm satisfied with the couple come ups to the kitty, if I would have just killed him like Bygtyme wanted me to I would of missed out on the opportunity to get some of my money back he took. You can't run around Philly robbing shit, doing dirt and not think it'll come back your way, this is what we call pay back!

I'm sitting on the side of the road not far from the address I had on Dame trying to figure my next move, I could take the money I got pack a bag and get low or I could give Bygtyme his money back take the money I got and get low and say fuck Dame or murder this motherfucka collect the rest of my money from Bygtyme and disappear, yea I think I'll stick to the script handle this business and move to Cali or some shit! In mid thought my phone rang

RED: Who this
Ebony: It's me, how'd you make out?

Yes, Dame baby mom on my line so called checking on me! I don't trust this shit but I play along just to see where it's going

RED: I'm good, everything was a go but I let him get away
Ebony/Bm: Well I've been hearing a few things you know
the streets talk

So I set and listened as Dame kids mother proceed to line him up and tell me all his info, she went on to tell me that the out of town shooter Dame hired was the one that shot me that night up Chew Ave. I never found out who did that shit but I figured Dame had to have part in it now I know for sure, she also told me that Dame knew it was me taking his spots running down on his shit, she said he called her and accused her of setting all that shit up she say he threatened to kill her now she want my help,

Ebony: Do you think we could meet somewhere and talk?
RED: So you can try and set me, Dame probably listening in on this call, naw sis I'm cool
Ebony: C'mon don't do me like that, I'm trying to help you, do you know what he would do to me if he knew I was even talking to you, please believe I don't play like that, this is important life or death, I have information that could benefit us both.
RED: Ok, when and where? But I'm telling you if shit doesn't feel right, I'm rocking out on everybody
Ebony: Trust me, help me, and help you

Of all place's she suggest we meet at LOVE PARK I guess she'll feel safe in the middle of center city or she feel like that's the last place Dame will be. I agreed to meet her at 8:00 but I plan on being there around 7:30 so I can set up and peep the scene I never show on your time I don't know rather to trust this chick or rock her too…

CHAPTER 12

When I finally left LOVE PARK my mind was twisting some of the things Dame's BM told me had me tripping a lot of the shit I knew or heard about but she went deep, real deep she told me where Dame mother rest her head, she said that she was there in the other room the day Dame was talking to the FEDS giving government names, nicknames and last known addresses she also told me that back when her and Dame was still together before I robbed her, Dame use to have her follow me around the city and watch my ever move said she was never actually there when he took my shit or robbed my workers but she's sure it was him.

I made it across the bridge to Camden NJ I got folks over there I can trust where I can get some rest in peace, without looking over my shudder or sleeping wit one eye open. I pulled on Kansas Rd in Fairview on my way to BLACK house, BLACK was this little bad half Rican jawn I meant a few years back ones we locked in that was it (She's a real one) she's been on my back about getting out of PHILLY come stay in NJ shit Camden ain't no different then PHILLY just different people, I do come over here often to get away, I get love in Camden, When I got to BLACK front door it smelled like Thanksgiving (She's always cooking) she got the music blasting that Hold on from NTG Redrum Records she opened the door wearing this all white cat suite wit a fat ass Dutch of that good gas in her lips, dancing enjoying life, when she seen it was me at the door she was hype, always glad to see me and me her, we hugged in the door way then walked in, she pasted me the Dutch and went in the kitchen I sat on the couch and relaxed my feet, about ten minutes later she came back to the living room wit another Dutch rolled and a plate of food, she hand me the plate then sat beside me on the couch

BLACK: "Boyfriend" how you been

RED: Hey baby, thanks for the food I'm starving, I'm good other then the basic bullshit how you doing? Looking good!

BLACK: I can't complain, tryna live my best life and stay out the way that's it! You know I hear about everything, what the hell you doing hanging out with that man baby mom? You just wanna piss him off don't make me have to kill this bitch I don't like her and I don't trust her.

RED: Naw it's not like that she been putting me on some shit, giving me some information on the situation and what not, I don't want her like that! I was going to fuck just to piss on him shit I might still I'm thinking about it

BLACK: Boy don't fucking play with me, I will fuckin kill both of ya'll cut your dick off

BLACK and I joked about the situation for a few I continued telling her all the shit EBONY told me and what I planned to do, I also told her I would be leaving town for a few soon, I asked if she wanted to go with me she replied "I wish I could" she let me know she had my back no matter what and her door was always open to me, she said she worry about me and that she's just glad that I'm going to step away for a while, she wished me luck! We sat and talked for hours about just about everything, it was like 2am when she got up off the couch and headed upstairs she looked back at me and said with this devilish grin are you cummin or not? I got up and followed. Upstairs BLACK goes in the bathroom to put on what she called night clothes but really wasn't much there (DAMN HER ASS FAT) I striped down to my boxers and wife beater and laid across the bed, BLACK walked around the room picking up clothes off the floor bending over just looking at her got my dick hard as a rock and she know exactly what she's doing! When she finally made her way to the bed I was ready!

That was some of the best sleep I had in a long time, I got up around 8:00 am BLACK was already up in the kitchen cooking breakfast I tried to slip out but she wasn't having it, she made me Turkey bacon, cheese eggs, home fries, toast, fresh OJ and a fresh fruit cup (THE REAL MVP) we sat and eat together I hugged her like I might never see her again and I was out the door. Headed toward the Ben Franklin Bridge I couldn't stop thinking about what BLACK was saying about Ebony far as her trying to set me up or what she's really up to. Do she really have a little thing for me and have good intentions, do Dame have a part in this, is it all part of the line up or do she feel safe wit me because she know I'm the one that's going to take Dame ass out? I can't figure this shit out but I will use the information she gave me to my advantage, I have to go check that address I got on his mother just to make sure! By the time I got to the Philly side of the Ben Franklin Bridge I had a bad feeling like something was off, I started to turn around and go back that's how deep it felt but I didn't drove right on into the city. My first stop is down 8th and Butler to pick up some money but after Ebony telling me they were tailing me around the city watching my moves I need to move a little different so I told the young bul to meet me at the bar at 8th and Erie Ave instead of on the block, after I leave there I have to go check on this address see who coming in and out of there, then I supposed to meet with Ebony she text me saying she want to see me, I'm thinking see me like what? I didn't say anything just agreed to meet her at this point it don't even matter this has got to come to an end somebody is going to die might be me, might be Dame, might be Dame and Ebony I really don't care just have my money ready when this shit done! My youngin walked in the bar looking shook he tells me Dame has been lurking in the area circling the block giving dirty looks, he gave me my money I told him he could take the rest of the day off, fall back and be careful, I left there and headed to my next destination some little block off of Forrest Ave and 74th soon as I pull on the block I can see Ms. Ann and her gossip squad on the porch I drove by real slow so I could get a good look but not be seen Ms. Ann knows me well like I said Dame and I use to be like family I would really hate to have to do something to his mom but shit getting serious! I stuck around for a few just to see if Dame might show up, I waited around for about an hour, NOTHING, I'll be back!

I text Ebony to see where she wanted to meet at, she didn't respond so I called her phone no answer, I waited like five minutes then called again, she answer but it sound as if she'd been crying so I asked was she ok, she acted like she couldn't talk, like somebody or something was stopping her from responding, then I heard a man voice in the back round it sound like she was being beat but I can't I really hear, then the phone hung up, now do I go past her house to see if she's alright or just wait for her to call back. Maybe Dame fond out his baby mom tryna sleep with the enemy and he in there beating her ass again, I don't know what to think but I'm not going past there if you want me call my phone!

I must have waited on that phone call all night but no call, so I went back on my mission!

CHAPTER 13

TIME IS MONEY

It's been over 24 hours and I still haven't heard a word back from Ebony I'm not worried like I care but I am curious to what the fuck happened to her so I called her phone and some older lady answered the phone I asked to speak to Ebony she said that Ebony was in critical condition she was beaten and left for dead her mom said that she was at Temple Hospital, I'm like "WOW" sorry to hear this and hung up, this dude tried to kill his kids mother! So I guess he know she's been talking to me, I have to take him down now before I fuck around and let him drop on me then all this was for nothing, naw I ain't going out like that, I'm on his ass.

I'm sitting in front of Dame mom house thinking the worst, I'm ready to run in her spot, tie her ass up make him come to me, I should of killed his ass a long time ago I had so many chances I was worried about money I let him get away, knowing what I know now after talking to Ebony I would of offed him from the jump, I gave him the benefit of the doubt I didn't know he was this far gone! Dame mom must be selling dope out the crib because it's sure a lot of traffic in and out but no Dame, I can't believe I let him get away, now he's on to me!

When I left Dame mom block I drove back Eastside to check on some money, I ran into little KEY brother, he ask me did I hear anything about who killed his brother (DAMN) he want blood, he not gone let that shit ride, he like if you hear anything Fam let me know! I'm like you know I'm on it, I got you, he shook my hand, hugged me and told me to watch my body, see in Philly when somebody tell you to watch your body you never really know how to take it, so I'm looking like ok Bro he walked away real slow, I'm like shit, that's a fucked up situation but I can't think about KEY right now, I have so much shit on my plate, he got what he got bottom line! Soon as I reached Price St Bygtyme was calling my phone (DAMN)

RED: Who this?

Bygtyme: C'mon cuz you playing, I need to be out of town tomorrow, game over, I hear you've been taring shit up playing cat and mouse with this dude now it's time to handle this business close this chapter

RED: Alright it's done!

I got off the phone feeling frustrated, mad at myself because I could have been done with this shit, now I'm under pressure but I always work better under pressure! I thought about it and decided it might be good for me to go up to the hospital and see what's going on for myself I need to know did Dame do that shit, did he send somebody and does she know where he is now, I picked up my couple dollars jump in the wheel and was out, I pulled up to Temple parked at

Germantown and Tioga got out and walked to the corner store, the Ave was live people everywhere, everybody trying to get at a Dollar I stood on the corner for a minute tryna get my thoughts together before I go inside not knowing what exactly to expect, I rolled my tree in a backwoods, blow one to the face, wait hold on either I'm high as shit or that's the same white Jeep Dame was driving last time I saw him, I needed to be sure, if so this is too good to be true, what he doing on this side of the map? Maybe he's checking to see if Ebony still alive, shit I don't know but I got him now, no games, fuck that money, time to put in that work! I walked up the block behind cars, peeking to see a face and yup it's him, I almost ran back to my truck I was so hype, I played it cool and walked fast, got in, started the engine and waited! There are always a lot of cops on Germantown Ave more so near the Hospital so I need for this dude to pull off.

About forty minutes pasted and we still sitting here, I don't care if it takes all night I'm here I'm not going anywhere until this is done, if nothing else I'm patient, I made the mistake of playing his game it almost cost me the whole deal, this time he will not get away! After sitting for an hour or so I see movement, look like some older lady is getting in the Jeep, that's not Dame's mother I know her. That must be Ebony's mom, Dame Kids Grand mom, the one I talked to earlier that day, shit I'm ready to hit the Jeep up with her ass in it, naw I'll follow and wait until he drop her off! Here we go, Dame pulled off slow, I waited a few seconds then I slowly slipped into traffic, I'm two cars back but I can see their every move, he took Tioga too Broad and made a left, he took Broad St. all the way down to City Hall so I'm guessing we're headed to South Philly or out South West, I took my gun out of the glove box checked to make sure one was in the head and that it was off safety. Then I made that call

Bygtyme: I've been waiting on your call! Is it done?

RED: I'm on him now, where can I meet you when it's done?

I need that bread so I can get the fuck out of here

Bygtyme: Don't call me acting cocky, handle that shit and hit me back! I'm around!

RED: Say less, I'll call you in about an hour or so

The white Jeep slowed down and pulled to the curb so I pulled over, I'm like half the block away so I can see and not be seen! He let the older lady out the Jeep at Broad and Tasker then continued down Broad I waited and then followed he hooked a right down Moore St. and kept straight(IM CREEPING) he pulled over up around 20th St. and sat in the Jeep, I pulled over mid-block and just watched.

A crowed of young bulls and a few girls were standing on the corner across from where Dame parked his Jeep, too much going on right here, dude got fiends running up on the Jeep traffic everywhere, so I wait! I'm out here in the heart of South Philly, in this dude hood by myself on some shit, I can feel it in the air it's going do tonight, Ebony told me Dame already had people on my head so I need to get him first and before sun rise I'm gone. Time past and it seem that the crowd was slowly fading, the traffic died down, I was sitting so long I got comfortable had to shake it off, I looked up and Dame was getting out the Jeep (I'm WOKE NOW) he walked back toward me headed to 19th St. I slide down in the truck to make sure he didn't see me, he walked right past me, I let him get like three cars lengths away before I got out the truck. Pulled my hood up on my head said a little prayer and it was on!

Remember this dude like 6 Ft 250 lb. me I'm 5Ft 9" 190 but with this gun in my hand we're the same size, I walked on the opposite side of the street with my head down, I wanna get close enough that the last thing he see is my face, I walked faster to catch up to his speed, I was about to move but it's people on the steps, I made sure they didn't see me I don't need nobody trying to identify me, as Dame crossed over 19th St. his phone rang (DESTRACTION) I crossed to the side of the street he was on and walked close behind him, he's on the phone talking reckless, I got close enough raised my burner and called his name! I didn't want to shoot him in the back, after all this shit I want him to see my face before I blow his brains out. When Dame turned around the look on his face said it all! It said "OH SHIT" I'M CAUGHT for a second I could see he was shook, didn't know what to do! Before I could squeeze the trigger Dame went for his gun, I busted two shots as he run between the two parked cars, he busted one back and ducked low, I threw two more shots and hit the car he was behind, I thought I hit him until he took off running, this big motherfucka trying to run I gave Chace, he turned the corner when I turned behind him he stopped and shot, my leg went weak almost fell but managed to stay on my feet, Dame dipped into an ally near 17th and Moore he know the hood better than me but I was on his ass, the more I ran the more I felt the pain in my leg, he ran thru the ally and out the other side, I followed when I came out the other end of the ally I started blasting, I saw Dame go down, he's on the ground but he's still alive because I can hear him screaming for help (DON'T BITCH NOW) it sound like he was on the phone, without thinking I ran over to the spot I thought he fell, I walked up on the side of the car first thing I notice was Dame gun on the ground I picked it up, second thing was a puddle of blood on the street where he fell, third thing he was gone! I stepped between the cars and out into the street, I was about to look under the cars when somebody started shooting from down the block, I can't see who but I returned fire, Dame must have been on the phone with his team, I'm in their hood, they got me running away from the direction of my truck, I'm hit in the leg (LEAKING) and I only have like four or five bullets left, I let one more shot go then ran toward Morris St. I need to make it around the block and back to my truck, I don't know where Dame went but I know he's hit bad, I made it to Morris St and stopped at the corner looked around and ran back up to 20th St and back around to my truck.

I crawled in my truck, thru the rearview I could see a crowd of people standing in the street and a body on the ground next to a parked car (THAT'S DAME I GOT HIM) everybody running around frantic on their cell phone yelling and hollering, somebody must have notice me because the back window of my truck exploded, followed by a hell of bullets, I ducked my head low and got the fuck up out of there, I keep straight on Moore St. until I hit the express way, heart racing like crazy, leg on fire but I made it out of there now I need to make it uptown to one of these Hospitals, gas them up so I can get this shit looked at and not go to jail, after that I'm to the crib to grab a couple bags meet Bygtyme collect my pay and I'm gone.

After all the rushing and pushing me I can't believe Bygtyme didn't have all my bread, he gave me 100,000 and said he'd have to check my later another time another state, I didn't complain because ones you have dudes like Bygtyme owning you, you will always be good! Plus I made out with close to a million buck playing in these streets, I survived, I never heard back from Ebony, I guess I'll see her around!

So yeah I know you'll probably wondering why I'm headed this way on I-95. Well let's say when you've been through what I've been through and you make it out you SURVIVE!! Best advice I can give is keep it moving; just keep it moving...

TO BE CONTINUED

Printed in the United States
By Bookmasters